To Golda,
who liked to climb trees, too

PARENTS' MAGAZINE PRESS, INC.
52 Vanderbilt Ave., New York 17, N. Y.

THE WONDERFUL TREE HOUSE

by Harold Longman
illustrated by Harry Devlin

Outside my house
There stands a tree;
An old oak tree
As big as can be.
One day I thought,
As I looked at the tree,

"Why, I could build
Up in that tree
The perfect house
For my friends and me!"

What a great surprise!

How they would rub their eyes!

"Gosh!" they would say,

"You must feel like a king

Up in that wonderful tree house thing!"

"Come up!" I would say.
"This is my place,
Come up and play.
There's plenty of space;
There's room to spare,
Here in my tree house up in the air."

But . . .

Would there be?

How much room *could* there be?

Come to think of it,

What kind of house

Should a tree house be?

A castle, maybe,
Strong and tall
With towers and
A high stone wall?
Why not?

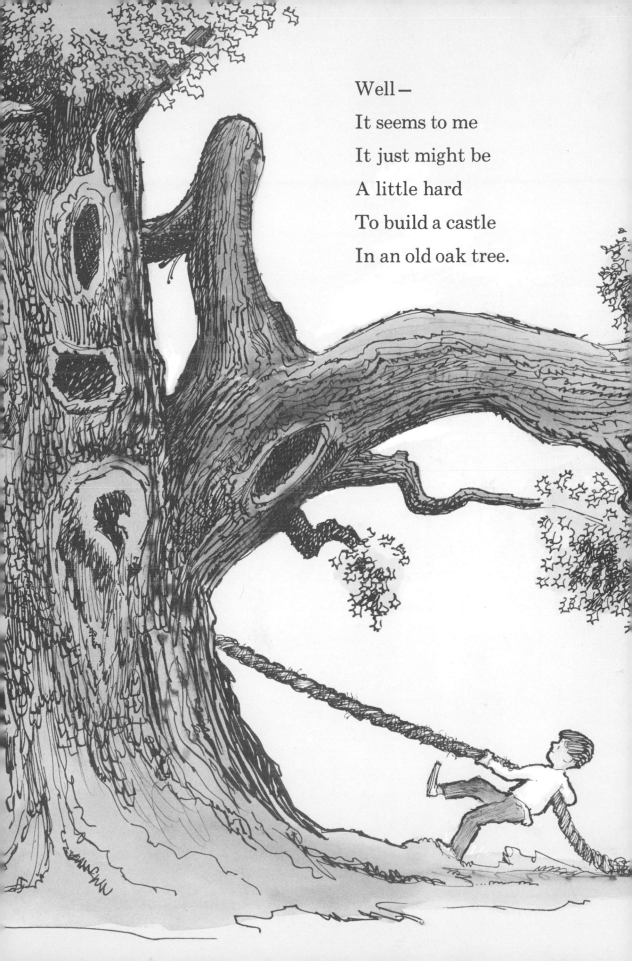

Well—
It seems to me
It just might be
A little hard
To build a castle
In an old oak tree.

Well, then,

How about a *little* house?

A fairy tale,

Hansel-and-Gretel,

Red-Riding-Hood

Sort of house?

Or... NO!

Not at all.
A little house
Is much too small.

Well,

If one is too big

And one is too little,

How about one

That's right in the middle?

So I climbed on a branch
And I looked around
At where I had been
Down on the ground.
I sat as still as a little mouse
And thought about my middle house.
Then I heard a *skitter-skat!*   *Skitter-skat!*
What's that?

A squirrel!

"Hello!" he said. "What's up?"

"I'm up," I said.

"I'm up here now

To build a house,

But I don't know how."

"A house?" said he.

"Why a house is as easy as can be.

Come with me!"

So I followed the squirrel way up in the tree.

Well!

You just can't guess what he showed to me.

A

great

big

old

hole!

What could I say?

What would *you* say?

"That is very nice," I said, "for squirrels.

Squirrel boys and squirrel girls.

But human boys need much more space;

Boys grow big in the human race."

A tree frog

Jumped down next to me.

A little brown frog

As brown as the tree.

"You want a house? Well, come with me!

A house is as easy as easy can be!"

I followed the tree frog
Up in the tree.
He jumped so fast
That I skinned my knee.
Did that stop me?
Oh no! I wanted to see
The house that the tree frog
Had for me.

"Here we are!" he said.
"It is airy and bright,
Not a black old hole
As dark as the night.
You can *see!* There's a view!
You can look all around
At birds in the sky
And boys on the ground."

What do you suppose he showed to me?

What kind of house did he have in the tree?

It was just

a

little

old

twig!   A little old twig

                About so big

                At the end of a branch

                On the old oak tree.

What could I say?

What would *you* say?

"It is very nice," I said, "for frogs.

Much nicer than the hollow logs

That other frogs live in.

It is airy and it has a view,

But for me it just won't do.

Frogs are little,

Boys are big,

Boys can't live on a little twig."

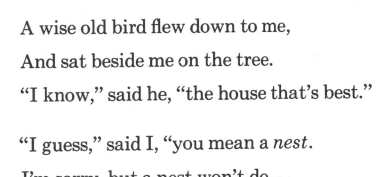

A wise old bird flew down to me,
And sat beside me on the tree.
"I know," said he, "the house that's best."

"I guess," said I, "you mean a *nest*.
I'm sorry, but a nest won't do—
Although I'm sure it's fine for you."

"A boy in a nest? How could you fit?
You couldn't stand or even sit.
Bugs and birds and frogs and squirrels
Need different homes than boys and girls."

"That's true," said I. "We both agree.
Then what kind of house should my tree house be?

"For a people house," said the bird,
"Ask people!"

I looked at the bird;
The bird looked at me.
I said, "I don't know
Any folks in a tree."

Said the bird, "All people
Once were small people.
Ask your dad."

My dad—gee! But would he? Could he?
"Ask," said the bird
And off he flew.
So I went to ask
You know who.

"You want a house in the old oak tree?

Why, that is as easy as easy can be!

Watch me!" said Dad.

He nailed some boards together like this . . .

And then he turned them over like this . . .

And nailed them up in the old oak tree . . .

To make a middle-size house for me.

Now how do you like my house in the tree?

It's all of the things I want it to be!

It's a castle

...a fort,

an airplane,

a nest...

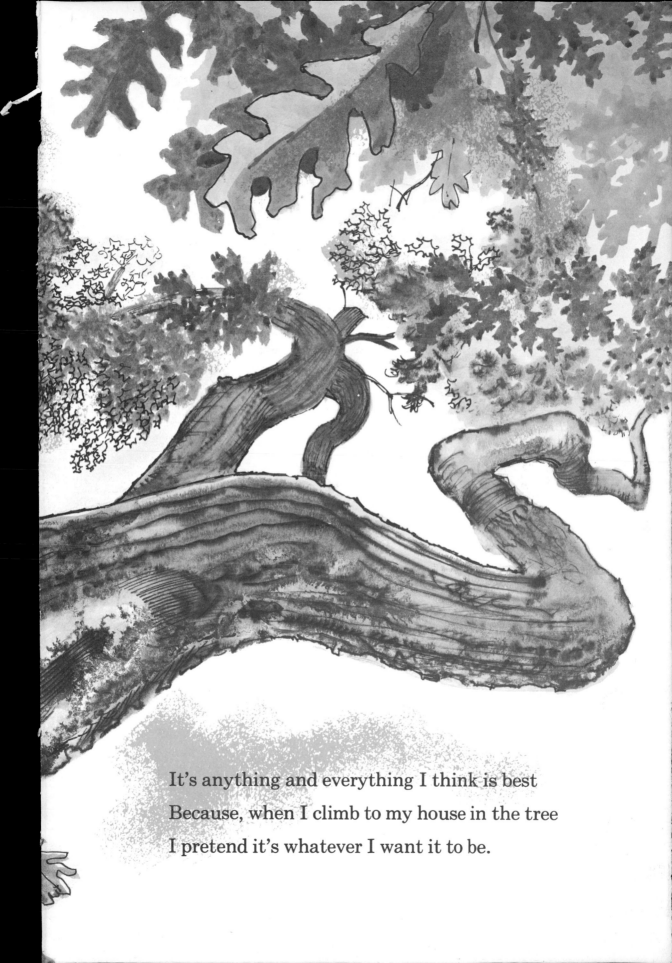

It's anything and everything I think is best
Because, when I climb to my house in the tree
I pretend it's whatever I want it to be.